A JOURNEY WITH GOD THROUGH THE UNKNOWN TO A PLACE
OF REST, REVELATION, RESTORATION AND HEALING.

IN THE VALLEY

SARAH NINHAM

Ark House Press
PO Box 1722, Port Orchard, WA 98366 USA
PO Box 1321, Mona Vale NSW 1660 Australia
PO Box 318 334, West Harbour, Auckland 0661 New Zealand
arkhousepress.com

Cataloguing in Publication Data:
Title: Revelations In The Valley
ISBN: 978-0-6480508-6-5 (pbk.)
Subjects: Christian Living,
Other Authors/Contributors: Ninham, Sarah

Design by initiateagency.com

Contents

Preface

Trial. What do we think of when we see the word trial? Perhaps it stirs up thoughts of doom and gloom, a negative experience, unfair, unjust, why me? But can it be a positive experience? I challenge you that, yes, in fact, the trials we face can be a positive experience. It may not seem like it at the time but when we come through the trial and look back, we often see the spiritual, emotional and physical healing that took place. What is the Bible's view on 'the trial'? Do we feel shame, condemnation and bad about ourselves because we perceive that we have done something to bring about the trial? Those questions and issues will be looked at from a 'God perspective' in this book of my personal writing and reflections as I experienced 'the trial'. Maybe you need spiritual healing, emotional healing, physical healing or psychological healing; whatever it may be, be encouraged through the words on printed page. I also pray that you will discover the breakthrough you need, whatever your trial may be.

2 My brethren, count it all joy when you fall into various trials, 3 knowing that the testing of your faith produces patience. 4 But let patience have its perfect work, that you may be perfect and complete, lacking nothing.

(James 1:2-4, NKJV)

Introduction

Valley. What picture comes to mind? Somewhere deep and inaccessible that will take a huge effort/ climb to get out of? Somewhere dark, lonely, cold and grey? Yes, these can all be visions of a valley – but and a big BUT – can a valley be a warm place of safety, a place of renewing, restoring and refreshing?

It can be both, as I found out through the valley I found myself in. But I learned that it was my perception of the valley that determined my experience in the valley. Our minds are powerful, powerful machines that determine our thoughts, emotions, actions; which is why we need to guard our minds so carefully.

Everyone's valleys will be different and we will experience different things/outcomes in our own valleys. Each valley is a deeply personal experience. But one thing is true; *Jesus is the same yesterday, today and forever (Hebrews 13:8, NKJV)*. He is with each of us in our valley. He will only make us walk with Him through the valley for as long as necessary, knowing each of our limits.

When I look back at 'my valley' and how it came about, I still find it hard to remember. Probably because I didn't really want to remember; too painful, too depressing to focus on it and relive it. However, sometimes we need to remember what happened in our valley to see how far God has brought us and how He brought us through something and to remember that He was always there with us.

This is what this book aims to do; to help us through our trials and see God in them rather than keep questioning 'the trials'. Then to rest, reflect and renew, coming out of the valley. This would become an important lesson for me in remembering how God brought me through and how He was always with me. He will never leave us in the valley; He will always walk with us and bring us through.

CHAPTER 1

Revelations In The Valley

The Valley

When I look back and think, 'How did I get to be in the valley? When did that journey through that valley start?' I think I was in it earlier than I thought.

I suppose it really started when I injured my back, over a year ago, in June 2015, chose to leave my job as a special needs teacher and went on the long journey of recovery. I had slipped and completely obliterated one disc in my lower back and the one above was bulging out and along with muscle wasting, my back was likened to a 65 year old's and a 'state' by my specialist. I was 38 years old.

I didn't realise back then just how long my recovery would take and what other trials I would face along the way. Just as well. When I look back I perceive that I had a positive approach to it all, and I did most of the time but also I can see how frustrated I was with it all, how frustrated with God I was, and with the whole situation in general really.

Little did I know that this was just the start of what unravelled into a downward spiral for my health.

As my back was recovering I felt God's leading in going to India to visit a school and orphanage that we as a family support there. I felt it would be good to give something back to God, in my time waiting for healing. A song at the time by John Waller, 'While I'm Waiting' (2014), really spoke to me with the words 'while I'm waiting I will serve you'. That was what was in my heart to do.

However, it materialised that while I was in India plans that I had didn't happen and the trip ended up being a place and time of rest, refreshment and healing for me, as I was slowed down to a halt basically. I also found myself giving messages across the remote churches, and found that my experiences with my back and with what God had shown me and revealed through scripture through the previous four months or so became the focus of these messages. None of this was part of the plan; but remember, we are just vessels and God can use anyone – we just have to be willing and surrender our plans in favour of His, as they are always better.

Anyway, back to how the next trial came about or should I say, how the trial continued on. I had been home from India around ten days (end of November 2015) and was feeling pretty good up to that point, but then boom! I found myself in the emergency room. I had awoken during the night with chest pain, tingling arms, faintness, shaking and involuntary muscle spasms; so many strange symptoms that I really hadn't a clue what was going on in my body. I made the call that I needed to go to the emergency room. In 38 years I have never had to visit the emergency room, so for me this was concerning with these symptoms. Hooked up to all the machines for several hours, it showed nothing unusual, every test showed 'normal'. Left confused and having daily symptoms at home, I really didn't know what to do. It was scary, lonely and I cried a lot when what I will call an 'episode' presented itself. Several episodes saw me calling my husband to take me to hospital as I really felt like I would lose consciousness at any point.

After back and forth visits to hospital, GP, etc, and having so many differing opinions on what it could be, I was really confused and disillusioned and just had to focus on trying to get myself better even though I didn't know what the problem was. 'Probable virus' was the only diagnosis, which could take six months to clear from my body and could have possibly left me with chronic fatigue.

The next six weeks or so saw me have continual fatigue, basically just sleeping and cooking and eating what I could when I could. I hardly left the house, had hideous vertigo so couldn't drive and just had to accept the routine and regain some sort of normality. This involved a lot of rest and doing everything I could to help myself and my body get over whatever it was I was fighting, because I was definitely fighting.

I had to move forward or I would have sunk even deeper into the valley I was already in and I certainly did not want that.

After another month or so, all the resting/nutrition seemed like it was paying off and I started to feel vaguely normal again. Maybe seventy percent of what I had been, which was good enough for me. So I started to plan. I started to look for a job, write, basically got busy with life again. I probably wasn't ready for all this looking back as a month into getting busy, like a slap in the face, I relapsed again back to the original virus symptoms and the chronic fatigue. This was April - four months since the first episode in December.

The focus of my symptoms the first time around had been on some virus I may or may not have picked up in India as there was really no other explanation for their strange constellation.

After the relapse it was like I wasn't taken seriously. This time I was just a hypochondriac. This I was not. The real symptoms were really happening and this bout of episodes saw me in and out of the emergency department two or three times during April. One time I couldn't even walk, but again – nothing – everything showed 'normal'. I then became 'chronic' and wasn't taken seriously by anyone in the medical world. Comments like, "whatever you have hasn't killed you yet, and is unlikely to" really weren't helpful. It would have been easy to focus on these comments and at times I did, which is when the 'it's all in my head' thoughts came in to my mind. Along with family/friends- 'it may be this, maybe it's that'-not really understanding what I was experiencing, wasn't helpful for me. Thankfully my true friend Vicki Matthews stood with me and had plenty of words of encouragement, just at the right time.

I started to realise that maybe I had missed the point of the first trial – busied myself too quickly, rushed too quickly back into the worldly rat race, instead of asking God where my focus should be. So I asked Him and He said clearly, 'You'. I should be focussing on me for the first time in my life and also remembering to focus on Him. Incidentally, this was, I realised, the first time I had stopped in my whole 38-year life. Properly stopped that is, and it felt good. The world would feed you the message that you can't just stop and sit there doing nothing but remember the perception of doing nothing is a perception. Doing nothing and letting your body heal and doing nothing but waiting on God is unseen to the average human but it is exactly what we need sometimes. It was certainly what I needed. Listen to God first as what he says is often not what man would advise and when we are perceived to be doing nothing, in fact we are doing everything.

But seek first the kingdom of God and His righteousness, and all these things shall be added to you. (Matthew 6:33, NKJV)

It was another two months before the fatigue finally went and I started to feel 'normal' again, something lifted and it was such a weight gone. I could walk twenty minutes again (believe me, that is an achievement compared to hardly being able to manage five), and I started to live again. But my thinking had changed this time. I was in no rush to get back to a job/ world view of what I should do.

The following chapters/penned words document the trial that I just briefly outlined. I have written of my thought processes, experiences, highs/lows and how I managed to get myself through the valley and out the other side, but not by my own efforts or the medical world but through revelations that God gave me as the trial unfolded and I walked through this valley with Him. Most importantly I have outlined the revelation of the lessons I learned from this journey and the application of these to my life.

Revelations

A week before my relapse (end March 2016) on a day I wasn't feeling well, after overdoing things, I was resting in bed and God gave me such exquisite visions.

- I saw a vision of a gold pen on a desk, while confined to my bed.
- I saw a glass lake, like the Tama Lakes in the Tongariro National Park not far from where I live in New Zealand.
- I saw a villa with a veranda with an amazing view of the lake and a pen to write scrolls.

The lake was like glass. The vision was exquisite and like a 'vision of heaven' which no words could describe fully. It reminded me of the scripture in Revelation where it talks about a sea of glass.

...and I saw something like a sea of glass... (Revelation 15:2, NKJV)

That is how I knew these were visions of heaven. Although these visions were wonderful, they also troubled me. What did they mean? Why was God revealing them to me now?

Then the relapse happened. What did this mean? Was I going to die this time? Anyway, a few weeks later I was listening to a sermon at church about the valley and the rod that will get you out of the valley. God truly spoke to me through this and there was an instant resonating in my spirit and revelation that in my valley, my rod was the gold pen I had seen in the vision from a few weeks earlier. It would be this gold pen that would get me out of the valley. At this point I felt God clearly tell me to 'write my way out of the valley' and that everything written (by the spirit) would turn to gold.

That same week my true friend, Vicki Matthews, sent me a lovely card (as always) with Psalm 23, again giving confirmation about the rod.

Yea, though I walk through the valley of the shadow of death, I will fear no evil: for thou art with me; thy rod and thy staff they comfort me. (Psalm 23:4, NKJV)

The rod and staff also signifies the Word and Spirit. That is how God would speak to me and subsequently how I would be able to write my way out of the valley.

Worship became a key part of my day in helping me to focus my time and energy on the right things. I was reminded that the valley wouldn't last forever through a song I heard.

The song '*Only For a Moment*' from Elevation Worship (*Here As In Heaven* album, 2014) really spoke to me and reminded me of the scripture in 2 Corinthians;

For our light and momentary troubles are achieving for us an eternal glory that far outweighs them all.

(2 Corinthians 4:17, NKJV)

The words of the song spoke about hope being an anchor for our souls in the storm and reminded me that I wasn't alone.

Reading daily scripture, each one on my bible app (https://www.bible.com/app) always seemed to be totally relevant to my situation on that particular day.

Still in the back of my mind – the whole vision of heaven etc - I read Philippians 1:21;

For me to live is Christ, to die is gain. (NKJV)

This gave me so much hope but also started me thinking. Why does God call some home early, some home late? I suppose we won't really know till we get to heaven but I came to the realisation that actually God must have an eternal purpose for us in heaven as well as a role marked out for each of us here on earth. It began to make sense to me why God calls us all home at different times.

In the busyness of life we don't often consider such things as it is so easy to focus our minds on our earthly home instead of our eternal home.

"For My thoughts are not your thoughts,
Nor are your ways My ways," says the Lord.
9 "For as the heavens are higher than the earth,
So are My ways higher than your ways,
And My thoughts than your thoughts". (Isaiah 55:8-9, NKJV)

The righteous perish, and no-one takes it to heart; the devout are taken away and no-one understands that the righteous are taken away to be spared from evil. Those who walk uprightly enter into peace; they find rest as they lie in death. (Isaiah 57:1-2, NKJV)

I felt God tell me to write my way out of the valley which I had to keep going back to in my mind so that I didn't lose focus and purpose. This would have been so easy to do and then God gave me the following revelation;

'Your words will remain even if you don't. They will live on and encourage many through their trials, give them hope, give them salvation, give them peace.'

On reflection I realised that the storm would pass. I would either be stronger here in this earthly home or the storm would pass and I would receive my inheritance. Whichever way it would be win-win and that was not for me to worry about, after all storms are only temporary.

Through this thought process I suddenly remembered that I had asked God for more time back in December, when I felt close to the end, an unexplainable feeling that I had never experienced before. I remember lying there in bed one day and just said, 'God, I'm not ready to go.'

I knew I wasn't in the right place, heart and mind, and I wasn't ready to meet my Father. I also knew back then that there was a book that I was supposed to be writing. I just didn't know what as God at this point had not given me the revelation 'to write my way out of the valley' (March 2016).

It started to evolve through the situation I found myself in, the valley I found myself in, and it continued to evolve and become clearer as I followed the instruction to write my way through the valley.

In this time of reflection and revelation I was also reminded of the literary events I had attended pre-relapse. I have always been a writer in my heart, having studied journalism, written a children's picture book and enjoying anything to do with writing. It is a God–given gift which I am thankful for. I could feel this gift stirring up inside me, even before 'the trial' and finding myself in the valley. The last time I had felt a big stirring of this gift was back in 2012 when attending a writers' conference, 'Written by the Spirit' in Shrewsbury, UK, where I met my friend Vicki for the first time.

I remember hearing the speakers at these events (February/March 2016) and the excitement and expectation from the nuggets of information that I gained. As I said, sitting there in these seminars I knew inside me that I was going to be writing a book, I just didn't know what yet as it hadn't yet been revealed to me. I was revisiting children's books I had written back in 2007, poetry and other random pieces of writing that I had written down. At least, I had organised them all into one place so I could try and make sense of what I should be writing! I started to think that I should write some sort of autobiography but didn't know why or how. Also in the back of my mind was India and if I was to be writing a book, when I discovered what that was, wouldn't it be great if I could make money out of it and the royalties could go to keep the orphanage running? That was in my mind when my husband and I wrote our first children's book. God puts things into our spirit and we have to follow that and try things out, being led by him, weighing up constantly – is this from God or from me?

After I received the revelation to 'write my way out of the valley' (end March 2016) that is what I did. I didn't have it all worked out, it evolved over time and the title for the book, *Revelations in the Valley*, came around two months later, just before I came out of the valley (May 2016). I wrote it down and that is what it has been called since that day.

The scriptures that joined all the dots as such for me were;

16 Therefore we do not lose heart. Though outwardly we are wasting away, yet inwardly we are being renewed day by day. 17 For our light and momentary troubles are achieving for us an eternal glory that far outweighs them all. 18 So we fix our eyes not on what is seen, but on what is unseen, since what is seen is temporary, but what is unseen is eternal. (2 Corinthians 4: 16-18, NKJV)

Through this trial I learned to listen to God and hear His voice. Often people wonder how God speaks and say they can't hear Him. We have to learn to be still and shut all other thoughts out, just focussing in on Him. He does speak and will speak, whether through worship, through His Word, through creation, through the Holy Spirit. He speaks to us all.

Be still, and know that I am God; I will be exalted among the nations, I will be exalted in the earth! (Psalm 46:10, NKJV)

This is easier said than done, I know, and in today's 24/7 world, full of technology at our fingertips, it is so hard just to be still. We think we are being still, but are we? When we do shut everything else out and allow ourselves to hear God, see God, feel God, this is when we receive revelations from Him. As I began to do this in the valley, I can truly say that I felt God with me and speaking to me each step of the way through my day. Whether through nature, a song, a scripture, whatever way; I started to seek these revelations and realised God is always speaking to us, it's just us who have had our ears closed for so long. I started to see God in the little things and it was good, it was refreshing. To step out of the busyness and experience this again was wonderful.

CHAPTER 2

Scripture Revelation

This chapter documents some of the scriptures God put in my spirit as I walked through the valley. Read them, be encouraged by His word and take what God is saying to you in your trial, through the words on the page.

It also documents my prayer response to God in the revelation of these scriptures, other prayers I offered up to God in the valley and some revelations that came through meditating on His word. Sometimes God would put a scripture on my heart, sometimes it would be the verse of the day through my bible app (https://www.bible.com/app) or a verse from a friend or sermon I heard. However the scriptures came didn't matter, it was God speaking to me and I had to listen and respond to those scriptures to enable me to continue my journey through the valley.

I will give you a new heart and put a new spirit within you; I will take the heart of stone out of your flesh and give you a heart of flesh. (Ezekiel 36:26, NKJV)

"God, give me a heart of flesh. My heart has become cold, refill me with your Holy Spirit and help me to see things through your eyes."

34 And He said to her, "Daughter, your faith has made you well. Go in peace, and be healed of your affliction." (Mark 5:34, NKJV)

'Thank you Father that You have given me faith; increase my faith and help me to believe that You can heal everything and that You can heal me.'

4 For whatever things were written before were written for our learning, that we through the patience and comfort of the Scriptures might have hope. (Romans 15:4. NKJV)

"Thank you for the comfort of your Word and thank you that your Word is sustaining me through this valley. Thank you for the hope that we have in You."

11 For He shall give His angels charge over you, to keep you in all your ways. 12 In their hands they shall bear you up, lest you dash your foot against a stone. (Psalms 91:11-12, NKJV)

"Thank you that You have your angels guarding me and thank you that your presence is with me wherever I go and your protection is with me at all times."

He who dwells in the secret place of the Most High shall abide under the shadow of the Almighty.
(Psalms 91:1, NKJV)

"Thank you that I can find strength in the secret place, help me to draw on You and thank you that You are protecting me day by day."

9 ...that if you confess with your mouth the Lord Jesus and believe in your heart that God has raised Him from the dead, you will be saved. (Romans 10:9, NKJV)

'Thank you for salvation and that salvation is available to everyone.'

3 Blessed be the God and Father of our Lord Jesus Christ, who according to His abundant mercy has begotten us again to a living hope through the resurrection of Jesus Christ from the dead, 4 to an inheritance incorruptible and undefiled and that does not fade away, reserved in heaven for you, 5 who are kept by the power of God through faith for salvation ready to be revealed in the last time. (1 Peter 1: 3-5 NKJV)

"Thank you that You have an inheritance waiting for me and thank you for your promises which keep me going through this valley. Thank you that You are walking with me through the valley even when I can't see you/feel You."

29 For our God is a consuming fire. (Hebrews 12:29, NKJV)

"Thank you Father that You consume every part of my being and that You can set me ablaze at the right time. Thank you for your power working in me and through me."

14 And the grace of our Lord was exceedingly abundant, with faith and love which are in Christ Jesus. (1 Timothy 1:14, NKJV)

"Without grace we are nothing. We can't earn it; it is a gift from You, God. Give me grace in this trial and in the bad days when my hope fades. Lift my eyes to you again and all that you have done for me."

11 But if the Spirit of Him who raised Jesus from the dead dwells in you, He who raised Christ from the dead will also give life to your mortal bodies through His Spirit who dwells in you. (Romans 8:11, NKJV)

"Thank you Father that You are in control and that my life is in your hands."

23 No longer drink only water, but use a little wine for your stomach's sake and your frequent infirmities. (1 Timothy 5:23, NKJV)

"Show me Father what to eat and drink and what to put in my body. Show me how to help myself and give me wisdom with my body."

And He said to me, "It is done! I am the Alpha and the Omega, the Beginning and the End. I will give of the fountain of the water of life freely to him who thirsts. (Revelation 21:6, NKJV)

"Help me to draw on You and thank you Father that I will never thirst, even if I feel thirsty in this valley You have provided me water to drink and You will finish it in your perfect timing."

In these times of reflection my mind went back to India (November 2015) and to the scripture that Pastor Johnson (founder of the orphanage, school and organisation World Wide People's Salvation Prayer Mission) had given to me back then.

4 For the Lord has chosen Jacob for Himself,
Israel for His special treasure. (Psalm 135:4, NKJV)

'God wants me for himself', was the word, like Jacob. In my spirit I knew what that meant – I was to be called home. I'm not sure why, something just resonated in my spirit when he gave me this scripture. This also reminded me of an earlier (June I think) card from Vicki where she said I was being airlifted by parachute. At the time my spirit said 'heaven' for some reason. That's when I started to think I was going to be called home soon. Obviously we will all be called home at some point, we just don't know when, only God knows the number of our days. The resonating that I was to be called 'home' is always correct as at some point we will all be called 'home' and it is a reminder of that hope and that this life is only temporary. It also reminded me that my soon isn't necessarily God's soon as the scripture says;

8 But, beloved, do not forget this one thing, that with the Lord one day is as a thousand years, and a thousand years as one day. (2 Peter 3:8 NKJV)

It was also a reminder that God loves me, I am special to Him and even when I fail, He will never give up on me and will always lead me.

Feeling alone and misunderstood in the valley, I was reminded of the scripture;

...For the Lord does not see as man sees; for man looks at the outward appearance, but the Lord looks at the heart. (1 Samuel 16:7, NKJV)

Man will let you down, that is a given fact. Doctors will let you down, friends, family will let you down/ not take you seriously – you will feel at the end of your tether – is it just me? Is it all in my head? But you know your body and know that it is telling you something. Take hold, God knows, He is holding you and He is the only one who will *not* let you down.

O Lord, God of my salvation,

I have cried out day and night before You.

2 Let my prayer come before You;

Incline Your ear to my cry.

3 For my soul is full of troubles,

And my life draws near to the grave.

(Psalms 88:1-3)

Crying out to God in these times, I thanked Him that my life was in His hands.

9 My eye wastes away because of affliction. LORD, I have called daily upon You; I have stretched out my hands to You. 10 Will You work wonders for the dead? Shall the dead arise and praise You? 11 Shall Your loving-kindness be declared in the grave? Or Your faithfulness in the place of destruction? 12 Shall Your wonders be known in the dark? And Your righteousness in the land of forgetfulness?

13But to You I have cried out, O LORD, And in the morning my prayer comes before You.

(Psalms 88:9-13)

Prayers to God

Every morning when my symptoms were at their worst and I was alone, deep in the valley, God had to be my first thought so that I could cope with/get through whatever the day may bring. The prayer that I offered to God in these times was;

"Today God, protect my vital organs – protect my heart, protect my brain, protect my lungs. Without you God I cannot breathe, You are ultimately holding me in your hands. Help me to remember that even when everyone else lets go and lets me down –

You, God do not. You are the ultimate physician. You designed me and made me, You formed my inmost parts while I was still in the womb. You are amazing. You know how I work and ultimately how to fix me. Thank you for doctors and their wisdom to help, but ultimately God, You are on the throne and in control.

Amen."

Seeming like I wasn't making any headway through the valley, worn out, frustrated and generally fed up in the valley, I started to contemplate.

Have I actually asked God to fix me? I thought I had in a round about way, but today I changed the focus. I prayed to God as such;

"God, You formed me in the inward parts of my mother's womb. I was perfect then; You made me whole and in your image. Restore my system to the default please. Just like when our gadgets go wrong, sometimes the only thing to do is to restore them to the default factory setting. Today, God, restore my nervous system, my endocrine system, (including diabetes) my cardiovascular system to the default working order that You designed for me. I don't know how to fix me, the doctors don't know how to fix me but You do. God, sort it. Get me up and going again, cycling and the freedom it brings, walking, enjoying life again, and show me what to focus my time on. I trust You. Amen."

I was still unclear in the valley and how I would get out of the valley-would I even get out of it? Is God calling me home or calling me to refocus my time and energy? Whichever way, those two grumpy days reminded me to praise God whatever the circumstances.

Writing my way through the valley was working but at times I struggled and thought, 'What's the point? Have I heard right?' But God reminded me of the purpose; that it would be a means to help the many people battling trials. Whether through illness, depression, fatigue, unanswered prayer, or should I say perceived unanswered prayer; whatever valley they find themselves in. It also became a means to me helping myself. Deep in the valley I would read my notes and they would help me through. It was like they weren't even my words and that I was looking down on myself in that valley and telling myself to 'keep going'.

Then came more revelation from God that I was on the right track.

'I will live on through your words. You may not see it now but the words of the pages you write are the seed that will be sown. You won't necessarily see the fruit in your lifetime but that doesn't matter —sow and obey My voice. The voice of I, El Hagyay (God of my life).'

The Lord will command His loving-kindness in the daytime,
And in the night His song shall be with me—
A prayer to the God of my life. (Psalms 42:8, NKJV)

I had been prompted to study the names of God through my trial and through a reading plan, '30 Names in 30 Days' by Dr. Tony Evans (www.TonyEvans.org) that I discovered on my bible app, so this is what I did. It proved a great tool in refocussing my mind and understanding scripture more fully/the nature of God.

I have listed the names of God that resonated with my spirit, the scripture reference for that name and in an order that can be said aloud to God as a prayer. A resource to refer back to that is a constant reminder that God is truth, He saved me, He is on the throne and without Him I am nothing. He is my strength, helper, rock, joy. He sees me, will provide all my needs and is always faithful.

NAMES OF GOD

Jehovah El Emeth - LORD God of Truth.

Into Your hand I commit my spirit;

You have redeemed me, O Lord God of truth.

(Psalms, 31:5, NKJV)

Jehovah Elohim Yeshua - LORD God of My Salvation.

O Lord, God of my salvation,

I have cried out day and night before You.

(Psalms 88:1, NKJV)

Elohim Bashamayim - God in Heaven.

And as soon as we heard these things, our hearts melted; neither did there remain any more courage in anyone because of you, for the Lord your God, He is God in heaven above and on earth beneath. (Joshua 2:11, NKJV)

Elohei Ma'uzzi - God of My Strength.

God is my strength and power

And He makes my way perfect.

(2 Samuel 22:3, NKJV)

Elohim Ozer Li - God My Helper.

Behold, God is my helper;

The Lord is with those who uphold my life.

(Psalms 54:4, NKJV)

El Sali - God, my Rock.

"The Lord lives!

Blessed be my Rock!

Let God be exalted,

The Rock of my salvation!

(2 Samuel 22:4, NKJV)

El Simchath Gili - God My Exceeding Joy.

Then I will go to the altar of God,

To God my exceeding joy;

And on the harp I will praise You,

O God, my God.

(Psalms 43:4, NKJV)

El Rai - God Seest Me.

Then she called the name of the Lord who spoke to her, You-Are-the-God-Who-Sees; for she said, "Have I also here seen Him who sees me?"

(Genesis 16:13, NKJV)

Jehovah Jireh - The Lord Will Provide.

And Abraham called the name of the place, The-Lord-Will-Provide; as it is said to this day, "In the Mount of the Lord it shall be provided."

(Genesis 22:14, NKJV)

El Emunah - The Faithful God.

Therefore know that the Lord your God, He is God, the faithful God who keeps covenant and mercy for a thousand generations with those who love Him and keep His commandments.

(Deutoronomy 7:9, **NKJV**)

CHAPTER 3

Therapy In The Valley

Nutrition

After the relapse in April 2016, my mind went more fully to nutrition. What am I putting in my body? What does my body need? What should I do to help my body through whatever it is fighting?

Apart from the undiagnosed symptoms/ virus/chronic fatigue in the background I had also been battling with chronic nausea for over three years, probably even longer, and at times it continually drained me.

I had discovered that bread and tea had been upsetting my stomach three years ago and my digestive issues steadily got worse and more and more things would make me sick. It was a process of elimination and discovering what was making me feel bad. I had never made the connection between diet and the nausea and vomiting symptoms but slowly the dots began to join as certain foods made me sicker and sicker. I eventually found that any product containing gluten would make me vomit; I had already removed most products but would still eat biscuits and crackers. So, after the relapse I decided to go completely gluten free and processed free and see if I could solve these issues, in case they were related. This thought was always in the back of my mind: 'Could all my symptoms be related?' But even if they weren't, a clean diet and nutritional support would certainly help me through whatever was happening in my body. I decided to invest in a good quality vitamin supplement, just in case I was lacking any key nutrients, which also came with a clean eating programme (https://www.bepure.co.nz/products/10-day-clean-eating-programme). I was pleasantly surprised at how simple some of the recipes from this programme were and also glad to see that I had been eating pretty clean anyway. This just gave me recipes for something a bit more filling such as pancakes, smoothies, more detailed salads, home-made dressings and clean treats to try. Rice flour, coconut oil, olive oil, berries and green leafy vegetables all became regular ingredients in my kitchen, along with herbs and spices including cinnamon, ginger and turmeric.

The following weeks saw me spending hours of my life searching the internet for clean recipes and this plan was enough to give me a good start on new recipes. Planning has always been a key part in cooking and shopping for my family so now I had to make sure I was planning for my own meals too. Keeping a food diary helped me identify if I was eating a variety of foods and food groups. Even though at first I didn't consider that it was making a huge difference to whatever symptoms I was facing, I am a reality girl and know that sometimes things take time and you don't necessarily see the results straight away. It was also a way for me to know that I was being good to and also supporting my body the best I could, so I didn't doubt myself and what I was facing. If I was putting in rubbish, I could expect to feel bad, but if I was eating well then I knew nutrition was not the issue.

Cutting down from two cups of coffee to one a day was surprisingly easy, and adjusting from filtered to instant came easily too. This was my one thing that I enjoyed-a filtered coffee in the morning and a filtered coffee in the afternoon-but to help myself I decided to cut back during this process, as after all it is considered a toxin. Apparently it has some health benefits and in low doses I consider it OK. It proved to me that actually if you want to achieve something you can. It's hard for our human nature to give up things we want, enjoy, perceive we need, but we have to listen to our bodies at any given time. I didn't want to do this I can tell you, but I decided that at this point it was what I should do.

Of course there were days when I got frustrated and thought, 'Look at so and so, they eat and drink what they like and are healthy and then look at me with my healthy diet but sick all the time.' I had to get past these thoughts and realise that God made us all different and unique and what is right for me isn't necessarily right for someone else.

A food is not necessarily wrong, it's only wrong if you 'have to have it', and it becomes an unbreakable routine/habit. We have to show that we can live without it and then it is OK. That could relate to a food, person, object; whatever it is, it should never become an addiction that we can't live without. We need to live addicted to God and other addictions we may have will cease.

At this time, when I was going through this nutrition journey and researching the best way to do everything I could for my body, I had been reading about the gut and how sometimes it gets damaged and the gut walls need strengthening and the gates tightening. Not long after reading and researching this I heard a sermon at church with a reading from Nehemiah 3 about rebuilding the gates and walls, which related to the blood and spirit, both of which need rebuilding.

This sermon really encouraged me and reminded me of what I had been reading and resonated in my spirit that that is what I needed to do; strengthen and tighten the gut walls and continue to do this through what I was already doing. This would stop any toxins getting through; just as in Nehemiah they were rebuilding the walls/gates to stop any enemies getting in and were building a wall of protection to regain their strength.

Again confirmation in this journey, that I was on the right track and

God was still with me and speaking to me.

I started to thank God every day that I was awake, breathing, living; thanking Him for the weather, family, being in New Zealand, remembering that this is the land He brought us to and how He gave us the desires of our heart to live in this country. I had to try really hard to focus on the positives of the day on my really tired/grumpy days. It is so easy to focus on what is wrong but that just digs us into a deeper hole. Don't get me wrong; I got it wrong and get it wrong all the time but we have to ask God to renew our thinking.

And do not be conformed to this world, but be transformed by the renewing of your mind, that you may prove what is that good and acceptable and perfect will of God. (Romans 12:2, NKJV)

Dog Therapy

We, as a family, have been totally blessed with our dog Yogi. Having her helped me through the dark times. As God knows what we need before we do, He knew ahead of time that I would need Yogi to help me through.

For your Father knows the things you have need of before you ask Him. (Matthew 6:8, NKJV)

Her particular breed (spoodle), character and nature were just what I needed. She became a sort of assistance dog, coming and nudging me, sniffing me, kind of warning me of something, even though I didn't know what. Often times I would test my blood sugar (being diabetic) and I would be low when she had nudged me. Never underestimate the perception of a dog! Yogi would come and hug me when I was having a hard day and exercise the love of the Father, the unconditional love that God gives to us all. God can use anyone and anything to speak to us and certainly did and does through our wonderful dog Yogi. She also became the inspiration for a dog blog which was my next form of therapy as I moved onwards through the valley.

Blog Therapy

Through Yogi being the character she is, I had the inspiration to start a dog blog (www.yogi1topdogbloggerlog.com). I can't actually remember the eureka moment but I went for it. I wanted to use my time in the valley to do something I enjoyed – namely writing. I may have been in the valley but I had the time, God gave me the inspiration and it became a great tool in helping me progress further through the valley.

I had no idea how to set up a blog. I knew vaguely what I could write and could visualise it; I just had to put this visualisation into being. This all happened pre-relapse (February 2016) as I started to gain some strength. I spent hours searching up how to start a blog and it became a huge learning curve for me. Even now, when I look back I wonder how I set it up and got it up and running. When God gives us inspiration we need to act in that very moment, that moment of inspiration, that moment of revelation. Some ideas are God-given; we just have to stop ourselves, talking ourselves out of it.

As I continued with the daily dog blog it became apparent to me why starting this was so important. It gave me a focus on both the good and bad days and something to keep me thinking and keep me going even when I wanted to give up and not write anymore – I didn't; I kept going. It became part of my day that sometimes I would think, 'What's the point?' But I believe God inspired my creative thinking in this new blog venture. I couldn't see any fruit of it yet, or know whether it would become a tool to make money and I had to block human comments out and remind myself that it was a God-inspired tool to get me through the season in the valley.

God also knew it was what I needed in this valley as writing is something I have always enjoyed. It relaxes me, makes me happy and I am most content with a pen in my hand! Yes, a physical one! God created me and He knows I like pens and as He revealed, there is a gold one waiting in heaven for me, which my mind goes back to often.

Deep in the valley I would say to God, 'I want the pen now', but knew deep down that the pen was not for this time.

Then I started doubting; would there actually be pens in heaven? On reflection, I knew there must be pens in heaven as the scripture says; names will be written in the Lamb's Book of Life. A pen is needed for that!

... but only those who are written in the Lamb's Book of Life. (Revelation 21:27, NKJV)

This was also a reminder to me, of obedience. If those writers back in Bible times had not listened to God and written down what God told them, the Bible wouldn't exist and where would that leave us today? It took this reminder of obedience to continue to write. God told me to write my way out of the valley, so that is what I continued to do and so the pen kept going with me through the valley.

All Scripture is given by inspiration of God, and is profitable for doctrine, for reproof, for correction, for instruction in righteousness, that the man of God may be complete, thoroughly equipped for every good work.

(2 Timothy 3:16-17, NKJV)

Let such a person consider this, that what we are in word by letters when we are absent, such we will also be in deed when we are present. (2 Corinthians 10:11, NKJV)

CHAPTER 4

On Through The Valley

When I finally started to see light at the end of the tunnel and felt like I may soon be coming out of the valley at the beginning of May, God reminded me of the scripture in James 5;

Is anyone among you sick? Let him call for the elders of the church, and let them pray over him, anointing him with oil in the name of the Lord. And the prayer of faith will save the sick, and the Lord will raise him up. And if he has committed sins, he will be forgiven. (James 5:14-15, NKJV)

I decided to do some research into this and found an extremely good commentary on the verse in Matthew Henry's complete commentary on the Bible, (Henry, M (2011) *Matthew Henry's Complete Commentary On The Whole Bible.* 1st edition [ebook] Christian Miracle Foundation Press, p.284338, 284369) outlined below.

This marked the beginning of coming out of the valley. It was the shift in my thinking, the shifting of my beliefs, my faith, and my trust in God.

This commentary spoke to me so clearly that I knew what I had to do. The commentary of James 5:14-15 is directly quoted as follows;

Excerpt 1:

In a day of affliction nothing is more seasonable than prayer. The person afflicted must pray himself, as well as engage the prayers of others for him. Times of affliction should be praying times. To this end God sends afflictions, that we may be engaged to seek him early; and that those who at other times have neglected him may be brought to enquire after him. The spirit is then most humble, the heart is broken and tender; and prayer is most acceptable to God when it comes from a contrite humble spirit. Afflictions naturally draw out complaints; and to whom should we complain but to God in prayer? It is necessary to exercise faith and hope under afflictions; and prayer is the appointed means both for obtaining and increasing these graces in us.

Excerpt 2:

However that be, there is one thing carefully to be observed here, that the saving of the sick is not ascribed to the anointing with oil, but to prayer: The prayer of faith shall save the sick ... prayer over the sick must proceed from, and be accompanied with, a lively faith. There must be faith both in the person praying and in the person prayed for. In a time of sickness, it is not the cold and formal prayer that is effectual, but the prayer of faith.

We should observe the success of prayer. The Lord shall raise up; that is, if he be a person capable and fit for deliverance, and if God have anything further for such a person to do in the world.

However, just as it seemed that I was getting my focus right and finally seeing a way out of the valley, I realised that something was trying to keep me in the valley. I had awoken feeling quite off, with an array of premenstrual symptoms, like a bear with a sore head, as the saying goes. I had to quickly find something positive to focus on or everything around me would irritate me-the house, my back, my tiredness. An uplifting worship song, followed by praying for my friend Vicki on an overseas trip, reminded me; it's not just about me and my circumstances, there are other things to focus on. When we do that, it takes our eyes off ourselves, onto God and what He wants us to see for that day.

Again, just as I had the revelation of scripture that I was finally going to get my way out of the valley, in the back of my mind a book I had read previously on chronic fatigue syndrome (Verrillo, Erica, (2012) *Chronic Fatigue Syndrome*, 2nd edition [ebook]) was playing on my mind. I had read parts of it as my doctor had given it as a possible explanation for my symptoms and I wanted to know more if this was what indeed I had been suffering with. Reading it had, at the time anyway, made me feel a lot better about my symptoms and that it wasn't all in my head, as there were plenty of people out there who had been through and were going through the same issues as me with no answers and not being taken seriously by the medical world. However, I didn't want to stay in this place just with a label, a diagnosis or to own it, I just wanted to get better.

Learning about the intricate workings of our bodies through this book made me feel better about all the symptoms. I considered that if I did have chronic fatigue (for this moment in time anyway, as remember God is God and He is on the throne) then at least I could stop trawling the internet looking for answers and a diagnosis for my confusing array of symptoms. At least then I would know how to pray too, I could continue with my plan of pacing my day, start to get back to some reality without worrying that I was doing more damage to my over-stressed body.

But still I remembered the scripture in James 5 and how simple it could be to get out of the valley. Sometimes our human brain overcomplicates things, we continually reason and think it is a ten step plan to success but it isn't, not with God anyway. He is not complicated. We are not in control, we could have 100 or two steps and still not get to success in our own efforts. He healed yesterday and still heals today. The world, and even some Christians, might say otherwise but there is plenty of evidence out there as well as this stated in the Bible:

Jesus Christ is the same yesterday, today, and forever. (Hebrews 13:8, NKJV)

Now as I was hoping that I was indeed coming out of the valley, my mind went back to my dreams. It is good to have goals and dreams and good to ponder on them.

My dream was to cycle once again. This was a hobby of mine which I enjoyed so much, and through it I could connect with God, be on my own with Him and enjoy the outdoors. When I injured my back it was a complete blow when I couldn't do this anymore. Then, my aim had been to be back on a bike by Christmas 2015. I took the advice; went to physio, the hydrotherapy pool daily, kept my positive attitude and the goal in mind to get back walking and more importantly back on my bike.

However, that didn't happen of course because of these additional symptoms, this trial and the so-called virus that put me in the valley. However, instead of looking back, I had to make a concentrated effort to look forward and look at how far I had already come in the year since the back injury. I remembered what a state my back was in a year ago: the restrictions, the pain, the limitations, the frustrations, the doctor's report.

Again, there had been so much confusion and differing opinions on the causes and how to best manage it etc. It would have been so easy to focus on this, however I decided to be proactive and get up and moving as quickly as possible – that was my aim anyway.

Whether my back injury was a contributing factor in the further downward spiral of my health or whether that was to slow me down to prepare me for this trial, bearing in mind how much I had already slowed down, matters not as I was not focussing on this. Going from being highly active with a full time stressful job, juggling responsibilities in the home, going on regular long walks over hilly terrain, twenty km cycle rides at the weekends, to only being able to walk ten minutes around a dog park with constant pain/niggles from my back, was no fun.

Something was driving me to tick loads of active things off my 'to do' list the previous summer (January 2015) and I am so glad now that I got out and about and enjoyed the great New Zealand outdoors. So I completed two things off my list-the Tongariro National Park and the Tongariro Crossing (one of the best one day walks in New Zealand), and the Old Coach Road cycle ride.

It's like I knew then that it might be a while before I could enjoy these things but at the time I didn't know why. Sometimes we have to do things while we are fit and healthy and follow the inward nudges as we don't know what is around the corner or what twists and turns we will come across in life.

In rehabilitating my back, I had to get out of my comfort zone and go to the hydrotherapy pool five times a week on my own, something I found really tough at the start as I really didn't want to go to a glorified hot bath full of 'old' people. I learnt to embrace it though, taking the wisdom of my specialist who suggested it as good rehabilitation. As I said before, God knows what's best and can give good advice through these specialists. We have to listen though! I had to go into that pool with God's eyes, speak to the people He brought across my path, people who I would never normally cross paths with if not for the injury. God always has a purpose in the places we go/find ourselves; often just to impart a word into someone's life. And often it is just that, 'a word', and that can be someone's beacon of light, hope and change in thinking.

So, as I have said, as I looked back, I could see now how my mind had been slowly changing in my attitude to 'the virus' and the valley that

I was still in.

The Joel Osteen word for the day – 'Today's Word with Joel and Victoria' (https://www.joelosteen.com/Pages/TodaysWord)-an online devotional that I read daily in the valley really resonated in my spirit and seemed to seamlessly tie in with everything else I had been reading at the time. The words helped me to stay positive and in particular the word that said in summary;

What you are facing is just a little setback, not time to give up, it's only one piece of the jigsaw that is missing and everything that happens will give glory to God. It doesn't mean game over because of the current restrictions.

As someone who is 'get up and go', loves the outdoors, discovering new places, etc, some days it was a hard pill to swallow that I couldn't do these things, but that was where I had to compromise. Instead I would sit in my cape cod chair with a view of the ranges, or sit on my chaise longue, take a short trip to the beach, all the little things I became thankful for. Or I could have focussed my energy on my circumstances and felt powerless, moody, frustrated and angry. I reminded myself that time is a great healer and that the doctor had originally said to give it six months, which of course being my stubborn self, I wasn't having back then. Now, however I realise that he was probably right!

At the time in January 2016 when he told me that, it seemed such a long time away but then I realised that it was already May and I started to fill with hope again. I realised I had already come so far through the valley and so my birthday in June became my focus.

God kept me on the 'hope' theme by giving me yet more hope through scripture and in particular through the Joel Osteen word on 6 May which was:

Therefore know that the LORD your God, He is God, the faithful God who keeps covenant and mercy for a thousand generations with those who love Him and keep His commandments.

(Deuteronomy 7:9, NKJV)

And then the verse of the day on my bible app. (http://bible.com/114/rev.1.8.nkjv)

"I am the Alpha and the Omega, the Beginning and the End," says the Lord, "who is and who was and who is to come, the Almighty." (Revelation 1:8, NKJV)

Confirmation on reasons for the trial

After reading the Joel Osteen word about the puzzle the other day, I saw God at work when I switched on the TV (this was 7 May) and there was Joel Osteen talking about that same puzzle piece. My ears pricked up and I quickly made notes to put it all into perspective and see God guiding me through this valley.

In summary the message said;

Even though the pain doesn't make sense now, it will fit in the big picture and make sense at the right time. The pain you go through will help you grow. Don't miss the lesson (something I was asking God the other day). It went on to say;

Don't just go through it, grow through it. You can help someone going through the same thing as you and encourage them through it. God can trust you with the pain, to get the lesson and encourage others.

Again, this brought me back to the reasons for writing the book and the instruction to 'write my way out of the valley'. This was confirmation to me that my valley would indeed encourage others who were going through similar experiences.

This was also confirmation that I was on the right track and had indeed heard God right. Sometimes we doubt ourselves and think, did I hear right? Is this really God leading? Let peace be your guide. It is so important I found, not to keep asking 'why' but to ask 'what' and always have your ears open to God.

This week of God's leading was the week that I finally got to see a specialist (9 May) about all the symptoms that had taken me to the emergency room on several occasions and had been six weeks in the making. My instinct was that God's got this, I don't need an appointment now but at the same time as I have said before sometimes we need the wisdom of doctors. I considered that even if it was a little blip causing problems then God would give the doctors wisdom to know what it is/find it/fix it to enable me to move forward in life.

The meeting with the doctor gave some relief and at least for the first time in this whole process I felt like I had been listened to. With a number of tests to undergo, I still knew there wasn't a quick route. To investigate and identify the adrenals and blood pressure as possible issues made me feel better as these things had crossed my mind before but no-one had ever looked into them. I decided to go with this, without letting my mind go to the negative in the waiting as it would have been so easy to do.

After this appointment I started to reflect on how far I had come through the valley, since first entering it in December 2015, and remembered a week or two earlier when I had asked God to restore me to my default settings, to restore me to how he created me. Since that time I realised:

- A wart on my finger, which I had had pretty much my whole life, since my teenage years at least, had disappeared! I had tried everything over the years and now it had miraculously gone. Now that might not sound amazing but it was one of those things that niggled at me daily. God is interested in the small niggly things as well as the big things. He can heal ALL things.

- My monthly cycle and other gynaecological issues that had niggled me for over two years suddenly improved.
- My blood sugar levels became excellent. They were good before but now they were excellent with fewer highs and lows.

Now, the dietary changes and nutrition (as detailed in chapter 3) may have all helped in this process. It is God who gives us the wisdom into what to change in our lives so that the healing can take place. Remember, our bodies are temples of the Holy Spirit;

19 Or do you not know that your body is the temple of the Holy Spirit who is in you, whom you have from God, and you are not your own? 20 For you were bought at a price; therefore glorify God in your body and in your spirit, which are God's.

(1 Corinthians 6:19, NKJV)

I got the call a week later (13 May) from the doctor to say that all my blood tests were normal, resonating with something that in the back of my mind that I had already known. So this was a relief, but at the same time still left me without answers. Again, I didn't want a label or a diagnosis; I just wanted to know what I could do/how to get well and how to pray if there was something specific that needed fixing. Then I remembered the prayer that asked God to reset my body to the womb default and kept going with that. I had to try hard not be negative and instead say; 'God, You have got this.'

The next day I was watching Lakewood Church: Joel Osteen on Shine TV and his message in summary was that:

Genes will come alive at the right time. God knew the things we would do in life, set the blueprint for us and releases our genes at exactly the right moment. Divine connections, ideas, are coming.

This really resonated with my spirit and kept my mind on God and not on what was happening in my body.

I started looking for the lesson in the valley I found myself in and I realised that I needed to set good habits with my relationship with God. My life was so busy before that I had little time to focus/seek God properly. I knew that I needed to make sure these new habits were deep within me so that I would be ready to face any challenges in life after I had got through this valley and considered that after all, that is all it is – a blip.

CHAPTER 5

Out Of The Valley

The coming out of the valley happened on 15th May during a church service. 'Don't miss your miracle' was the sermon. God prompted me to go forward at the altar call, to not walk alone anymore. I was anointed with oil, just as I had been reading earlier in the week; to call the elders of the church to pray and the sick person will be made well. (James 5:14-15, NKJV). This was God providing me with an opportunity and prompting to put my faith into action. I fell prostate and felt so at peace. I haven't often fallen prostrate before God but most of the fallings you read about in the Bible were prostrate and in response to something; revelation of God, something God had said, in repentance and awe of who God was, in crying out for an answer or direction, in seeking Him for something.

Scripture is full of cases where people fell prostrate in response to something in the presence of God. A few I have referenced here.

Then Moses and Aaron came in from the presence of the assembly to the doorway of the tent of meeting and fell on their faces. Then the glory of the LORD appeared to them... (Numbers 20:6, NKJV)

And when the disciples heard it, they fell on their faces and were greatly afraid. (Matthew 17:6, NKJV)

And all the angels were standing around the throne and around the elders and the four living creatures; and they fell on their faces before the throne and worshipped God. (Revelation 7:11, NKJV)

Abram fell on his face, and God talked with him...
(Genesis 17:3, NKJV)

In my case it was a crying out of, 'This stops here'. I was crying out to Him in that moment of the manifestation of His presence, responding to the call for someone to stand with me in faith at the altar.

I had been crying out to God, He had seen what I had been going through. Even when man doesn't understand or doesn't get you, God knows, God sees and God knows our hearts, our longings, our desires, and our needs. He knows why, how and when. Even when we think we are walking alone, we are not. God is walking right next to us but sometimes we need someone to physically stand with us in our faith for our miracle, our healing. The glory would go to God was the prayer; that many would come to know God through my testimony of healing and struggles I had encountered. This is where I had arrived in my thinking too. When we come to the end of ourselves, God moves, if we let Him, believe Him, cry out to Him. 'This stops here' had been going through my mind during that week and I came to the end of myself, fed up with the health issues, fed up of talking about them, fed up with thinking about them, fed up of that being the focus of my day, every day. God heard me; as He also hears you, loves you and WILL move your mountain at the right time. A song by Lauren Daigle called 'Trust' sums this up perfectly and it was a source of inspiration for me in building my faith in the valley. The song reminded me to trust God even when He doesn't answer instantly.

My energy finally came back the next day (16 May) and I could walk again for twenty minutes without staggering, limping or being exhausted. This was truly exhilarating, like I had come back to life. I could drive again, after not being able to for six weeks or so, and I felt a huge weight was lifted. It happened overnight basically, after the prayer it was almost instant, suddenly I was better and was out of the valley. It was all thanks to God and the healing journey that He had taken me on over the previous months. This made me realise that it is so important to respond when God calls or we could miss out on so much.

Just as this breakthrough happened and I was out of the valley, my hideous nausea, that had faded into the background for nearly a couple of months after the dietary changes I had made (chapter 3) had improved my symptoms, returned.

I looked for the positives; at least my body didn't go into a fight response like it used to after ingesting something that my body couldn't tolerate. But still, the heightened nausea was hard to ignore and tried to rob me of my healing of the other symptoms. At the time this started again, I had been told by several doctors that I could have possible slow emptying of the stomach due to the nausea/diabetes, which would probably explain the symptoms. However, despite still having more questions than answers about these returning symptoms I had to try and focus past this and make sure that it didn't send me on a downward spiral in my thinking but still believe God and believe that He can cure all things. Whenever I had received prayer for healing in this valley I had focussed on asking God for the hideous virus and chronic fatigue symptoms to go, but forgot about the gastric issues. We have to be specific with God – yes, He knows what we need before we ask but He wants us to ask, be specific and remember that He is the God of miracles and that He is on the throne.

For your Father knows the things you have need of before you ask Him. (Matthew 6:8, **NKJV**).

Nothing is impossible with God. Sometimes the answer isn't in our timing or the way we think it will come, but it will always come, somehow. The key is to still praise Him in the good times and the bad.

On coming out of the valley, I wrote down and reflected on what had now changed in my life and reminded myself of what God had done for me.

- Chronic fatigue - gone
- Feeling faint/episodes - gone
- Vertigo - gone
- Can walk twenty minutes +
- Can drive again
- Can sit and rest but out of choice

This reflection was just as I had done previously, after asking God to restore me to my default settings. This continues, even now, to be an ongoing process and it is so important that the reflections continue to be an ongoing process too.

Even though I experienced gastric problems during this week where I saw the healing for the other things, I still believed God and had to believe that He was going to sort this biggy of the last three years out. God was in the process of fixing me, inside out; I just had to trust Him in the process and use the wisdom He continued now to give me in what to eat, what to do, what not to do; when to rise, when to sleep, when to stop, when to go. I had to ask God for the wisdom in how to spend my days. My mind started to rush ahead, looking for a job, doing things, general busyness, but I knew God was saying;

'No, stop! I am giving you this time to reset and refresh.'

And, all the time I was remembering the gold pen revelation and the prompting to write the workings of this trial down. I had discovered, while in the valley, that there were many people out there facing similar struggles to me. This realisation came through conversations with friends and acquaintances who were experiencing health issues; hearing stories of struggles on the radio and TV; coming across people on my daily walks and also online through my research of my symptoms. God can speak through any of us and through our trials; we have to be obedient to how God wants us to work through our trial.

I had already prayed for God to promote my husband and give us enough money so the pressure was off me to work in this season, and in this God was faithful and answered. So why was I, now I was coming out of the valley, striving to think I should be out working? God can clear the debt; it was me just not believing that fully. God wasn't the problem; it was me and my unbelief. He has unlimited resources available to me and holds the key to the biggest bank in the world. I considered; have I actually asked God for any of His provision?

As I got better the first time around (February 2016), I had told God my dreams and desires ultimately to be a writer. He helped me to set up the blog and get this written; I just had to continue to trust Him to lead me in these writing ventures. Still unsure of the exact purpose, what it would achieve and what I would do with it when it was finished, all I could do was give it over to God. Only He knows the future; I am not in control of that, but one thing I did know was that He had told me to 'write my way out of the valley', so I continued to do so in obedience.

Looking Back

At this time of coming out of the valley, I started to replay everything that had happened on my journey through this valley.

I went back in my mind to my back injury and leaving my job in September 2015; I was going to get back on my feet as quick as possible, get a job again, and ride a bike again. That didn't happen and God had told me, as I was coming out of the valley, to slow down and not to be so hasty about these things.

He prompted me to go to India, so I did. I went, came back, got sick and thought to myself, 'That was not part of the plan.' I got better, started writing, started looking for a job again, got sick again as I have documented before.

Getting sick the second time, when I look back, was probably easier, as I had a clearer idea how to cope/ manage my symptoms and knew I got better. But at the same time I didn't want all that again, all the symptoms, limitations, pain, frustration. It became an emotional roller coaster at times and I really did question God at times, doubt myself, blame myself, wonder what I was doing wrong. In these times it is so important to seek God and NOT man as so often this can make us feel worse. Everybody can have so much advice for us but ultimately we need to listen to God's advice – what is He saying in all this? Sometimes we need the isolation to connect properly with God. Jesus often withdrew himself to a remote place to pray and be alone with the Father.

So He Himself often withdrew into the wilderness and prayed. (Luke 5:16, NKJV)

That is when I feel closest to God, when I am alone, out in a remote spot in His creation, walking, talking, refreshing, renewing. Cycling used to be my escape for this alone time so it was hard not being able to.

Keeping the aim and hope of one day doing it again though, kept me going; having that Godly confidence and perseverance.

And in the meantime, connecting with God in a different way and place. Whether it was sitting on my chaise longue, walking the dog, a walk around the lake; that didn't matter. The important thing was that I could feel God with me wherever I went and felt continually connected to Him. I became excited and expectant of what route He may lead me on which reminded me of a card that my friend Vicki gave me; 'The best routes are the ones you haven't ridden.' So true. Even though everything was not solved, the main virus which nobody could fathom or diagnose, was finally gone.

Coming out of our valleys are a time of celebration but also are not always plain sailing as I found. Having been in that dark valley for so long, in that place of the unknown, suddenly coming out of it was amazing. We have to, as I had to, quickly grab hold of what has happened, thank God and move forward so that we don't slip backwards into that valley.

Life will be full of valleys, that is a given and just part of life and we never know when the next one will come. That matters not. The important thing is what we do in the valley and most importantly what we do with our minds when in this place, ensuring that we keep focussed on Him and not the circumstances.

You will keep him in perfect peace, whose mind is stayed on You, because he trusts in You. (Isaiah 26:3, NKJV)

Write

In my case, it was writing – I was to write in the valley. I knew that, God had told me that at the start; to 'write my way out of the valley.' Without that clear guidance I really don't know how or when I would have got out.

In the process of coming out of the valley I knew time was pressing on and something was telling me to get this book written, that I didn't have much time (whatever that meant). But at the same time, I was saying, 'God, what is the outcome? What is the end? What is the focus now for this book? Is it complete healing and glory to God or a calling home?' Whichever it was, I knew it needed to be finished for others to benefit and for me to move forward either in this life or the life to come.

It was a lonely process at times and I got frustrated when I felt those closest to me didn't understand; the gastric issues, vision for the book and me in general, but we have to remember that ultimately God is first and what He thinks is what really matters. He is the only one who will love us unconditionally, not judge us, not ignore us and truly care for us. Each of our journeys and ways out of the valley are unique, and others may not understand, but fix your eyes on God.

As the scripture says;

If God is for us, who can be against us?
(Romans 8:31, NKJV)

We so often beat ourselves up when we get frustrated and are so hard on ourselves – why do I act like that? That is so unholy; then we feel guilty and bad about ourselves. When we look deeply, we actually find that many of these feelings come from what other people think, not God's view about us. He understands that we are human and wants to help us through these difficult times. It's not wrong to feel down, deflated; these are normal human emotions. As God said;

Be angry, and do not sin... (Ephesians 4:26, NKJV)

We just have to give these emotions to God daily so they don't control us.

For God has not given us a spirit of fear, but of power, and of love and of a sound mind. (2 Timothy 1:7, NKJV)

CHAPTER 6

Don't Miss The Lessons

Sitting out on my cape cod chair, I was reminded, 'Don't miss the lesson.' As my health began to improve my mind started to get busy, it started to get ahead of itself. I have time now, what can I do? What should I be doing?

I felt God clearly speak to me:

'Stop, look and listen, enjoy Me, enjoy My creation, enjoy writing and reach out to those in need.'

'Be a light, enjoy your motherly duties, look after your husband, and be there for your children. Forget work for now.' (In the sense of earning money, working for someone.)

Last time I got sick I said to God, 'I am a writer, I want to write for a living, you have put the gift in me, give me the desires of my heart.' I started the blog, went to literary festivals and pursued my desire to write. I was at peace writing and had come up with a good writing plan, but in the back of my head, I was wanting to earn money. It is our unbelief that stops our dreams. We ask God and then doubt Him. What is the blueprint for life? Nine to five work, slog, grind and misery; continual reasoning or listening to God? We often have to step out of our comfort zone to hear God, listen to Him and obey by moving.

Feeling guilty for sitting/resting is always something I have struggled with but God knows what we need in order to hear Him and not be distracted by busyness. He knows how we function and process. The world would say, 'You can't just sit there idly writing. What are you writing for? What's it going to achieve?' But God says, 'Yes you can.' We are not accountable to man, only to God. God was saying to me at that particular point on my journey, to establish good habits with Him, to be obedient with my writing, to manage my thoughts by having joy and to live in joy.

On reflection I saw a four-part lesson start to emerge.

THE LESSONS

1. Stop, look and listen (to what God is saying/showing).
2. Establish good habits (in relationship with God through prayer, scripture, worship).
3. Live in joy.
4. Rest, reflect, renew – (however that may be – for me writing).

Documented in this chapter will be how I realised these lessons and my reflections of all that God had been teaching me in the valley.

1. STOP, LOOK AND LISTEN

For me, to live is Christ, and to die is gain. (Philippians 1:21, NKJV)

As I have said, this verse became very real to me in this trial, and probably for the first time I really understood what these words mean. When hope is lost and you are unsure of where your life is going – in my case, will I keep living or will I die from these undiagnosed symptoms? –

that verse gave me the hope I needed to carry on through. We often read and quote the Bible but do we really take time to study what the words on the page mean? Or even read the scriptures, learn them and meditate on them? In my case, often not. Sometimes we only come to know the true meaning of God's words through circumstances we go through at a certain time. That is why it is so important to really know what the Word of God means and to plant it deep in our hearts so that in times of trials we can recall it. In that valley, in that dark place, the scripture we have meditated on in our lives will come flooding back.

We belong to God. God controls whether we live or die. God has appointed for each of us a time and a plan on earth to fulfil His purposes. That puts life into perspective.

When I told people that I wondered if this is the end, many may have thought I was overreacting, was a worrier, over-anxious, a hypochondriac, depressed; these were all lies that the devil would try to use to feed my mind; but I was none of these. My symptoms were real and I see them now, on reflection, as a wake-up call to 'stop, look and listen'; time to take a look at my life and implement change that needed to happen so that God could mould me into who He created me to be.

2. ESTABLISH GOOD HABITS

Time-not enough, juggling it-can be a big stealer of joy and can hinder us from experiencing the joy that comes from being in His presence. But at the same time I realised that God is not timing us either as it is our choice whether we choose to spend time with Him and for how long. We need to get away from this; thinking that there is an exact amount of time we need to spend with God and an exact amount of time before we can experience His presence. God doesn't want us to rush in and out of

His presence but at the same time He is not sitting there with a stopwatch either. Focussed time and energy knows no time limit. I have gone outside to pray in my chair before and thought only five or ten minutes went by, but came in and in fact forty minutes had passed. Time in His presence is not measured by earthly time, it is timeless. We often rush, saying, 'I only have ten minutes, twenty minutes', whatever it may be and constantly look at the clock. In these times we are in fact not really focussed on Him and His presence. Quality should take priority over quantity. I am totally guilty of this and always thinking of the next thing but God says;

'Stop! Give me the time you have and I will turn it into something wonderful. I will refresh you spiritually, emotionally, physically and renew your mind and thinking for this day. You need energy, I have it. Yes, that coffee will give you a boost but the boost of the spirit is so much better.'

Putting on some timed worship music helped me to focus so much. If I had half an hour I would make a playlist half an hour long so I didn't have to keep looking at the clock and the music would refocus my attention. Don't get me wrong, I don't always do this and have to constantly guard against forgetting the lessons I learned in the valley. When I don't take time to focus in on God my Father, my times are rushed, I feel rushed and stressed and my joy could so easily be zapped. Find what works for you, do it and stick to it, commit to it and see the results.

Be encouraged by these scriptures and live in joy!

For His anger is but for a moment, His favour is for life; weeping may endure for a night, but joy comes in the morning. (Psalms 30:5, NKJV)

The joy of the Lord is your strength.
(Nehemiah 8:10, NKJV)

But the fruit of the Spirit is love, joy, peace, long-suffering, kindness, goodness, faithfulness, (Galatians 5:22, **NKJV**)

You will show me the path of life; In Your presence is fullness of joy; at Your right hand are pleasures forevermore. (Psalms 16:11, **NKJV**)

Restore to me the joy of Your salvation, and uphold me by Your generous Spirit. (Psalms 51:12, **NKJV**)

My brethren, count it all joy when you fall into various trials, knowing that the testing of your faith produces patience. (James 1:2, **NKJV**)

And the disciples were filled with joy and with the Holy Spirit. (Acts 13:52, NKJV)

These things I have spoken to you, that My joy may remain in you, and that your joy may be full. (John 15:11, **NKJV**)

Yes, brother, let me have joy from you in the Lord; refresh my heart in the Lord. (Philemon 1:20, **NKJV**)

You have made known to me the ways of life; You will make me full of joy in Your presence.' (Acts 2:28, **NKJV**)

3. LIVE IN JOY

The word joy and the word trial don't seem to belong together in the same sentence but they did join hand in hand in my trial.

The reality of what joy is became very real in my life through this trial.

Weeping may endure for a night but joy comes in the morning. (Psalms 30:5, NKJV)

Coming through the valley, the revelation and manifestation of God's joy washed over me in such a real way, in a way I had never experienced in my life before. Probably the only time I had felt this joy was on first being saved, so I remembered.

Restore to me the joy of Your salvation,
And uphold me by Your generous Spirit.
(Psalms 51:12, NKJV)

It's so easy to get away from God's joy with the busyness and stresses of life. On realisation that I should be living in joy daily, I would wake feeling refreshed, joyful, and alive. It didn't matter what the weather was doing, what the circumstances were, what the bank balance said, I got up and thanked God I was breathing, thanked God for my life, and thanked Him for any number of seemingly little things in my life. It wasn't a forced thing but completely natural from within my spirit. The point of sharing this is that one month into walking out of the valley, I started to feel my joy was dwindling and the stresses of life starting to creep back up. I was in danger of missing the lesson to 'establish good habits', to 'live in joy' and also forgetting all that I had learned in the valley. This is the test I suppose; can we transfer what we learned in our valleys into real life, especially when life seems to be going well?

We have to say a big *no* to busyness and stop, look and listen, not let good habits be stolen otherwise the stresses of life creep in and steal our joy, exactly what the devil wants.

The joy of the Lord is your strength.
(Nehemiah 8:10, NKJV)

That scripture became very real to me and is firmly stuck on my wall. Given to me by friends in India, at the time I didn't know how important that scripture would become and that I would read it every day and be reminded that indeed – the joy of the Lord is my strength.

4. REST, REFLECT, RENEW

Now, through this time coming out of the valley and making sense of it all and applying the lessons I had learnt, I continued to receive all that God had for me.

Listening to a visiting speaker (John Cairns) at church on 26 June 2016, the main points of his message were exactly where I had got to in my thinking and his points instantly resonated with my spirit and were such an encouragement to me. In summary, the main points which stood out for me were;

- *Desperate people get miracles.*
- *It is ultimately our faith not the person praying for us that gets results while*

they stand in agreement with us.

- *We don't know why the trial comes but how we approach it and live with it is what shows our true commitment and how deep our faith in Him lies.*
- *We have to thank God for the things that are good and say, 'I believe you God – You have this under control', even when you can't see it.*

This was confirmation that the trials we face are not our fault and was just what I needed to hear. Often the devil puts this lie to us so we take this line of thinking and so the devil steals our peace and joy. Here speaking at church was a mighty man of God who had been through all sorts of sickness himself, but was still standing and thanking God even though it didn't make any sense. It is not our job to make sense of everything, our job is to trust God and have an active faith.

Trust in the Lord with all your heart, and lean not on your own understanding; in all your ways acknowledge Him, and He shall direct your paths. (Proverbs 3:5&6, NKJV)

Remembering all the times when our faith was active in previous circumstances is a great tool to reactivating our faith. List all the times you acted in faith and how God moved in your life and also look in the Bible, full of testimonies of faith too.

My own reflection of active faith took me back to the time that I trained to be a teacher and the time that we moved to New Zealand. That was faith in action, looking back, and it all tied together for the good plan God had for us.

And we know that all things work together for good to those who love God, to those who are the called according to His purpose. (Romans 8:28, NKJV)

I never wanted to be a teacher when I was young, I was a writer at heart and studied journalism. I always said the one job I would never do was be a teacher! Now, 'never say never' and be careful what you say you will never do! I had ideas; God had other plans for me and at 32 I was led to train as a primary school teacher, not knowing where this would lead and not an easy road to go down. I found myself working with special needs children. This was also never my intention but was obviously God's plan for me.

My husband Paul and I had always had, at the back of our minds, a desire to come to live in New Zealand and when I was in the middle of my teacher training back in 2010, this dream came to the forefront once again. We knew in our spirit that this was God as both had the dream pop back into our hearts at the same time, independent of the other. In 2011 we decided to go and 'spy out the land' as such and test the call. Was New Zealand really for us? Was this God's leading? We went on a ten-day whirlwind tour of New Zealand feeling before we went that we should base ourselves on the west coast. God paved the way with accommodation, etc, and we found that we instantly felt at home, a strange feeling never felt anywhere else before, even in the UK.

Now dreams don't always come to pass instantly, as we found. It was another two years before we actually moved to New Zealand and everything we did in that time worked towards that goal. We sold our house in 2012 and a good proportion of our possessions, and moved into rented accommodation, which incidentally we thought would only be a matter of months but turned out to be for sixteen months. We got to the point where we were doubting, as it looked like we had heard wrong and that the dream wasn't going to happen at this time. However we pressed on and decided in faith to book our flights in January 2013 for 30 July that same year. We thought we would have jobs by then and if not we would pack up and go anyway as it would be easier to get work if we were there on the ground.

July came, we didn't have jobs but we were believing God. So, we packed everything up and said goodbye to the UK with just one suitcase each, leaving our other eight boxes of stuff with friends, got on a plane and went, us and our two children, Peter then 11 and Abigail then 9.

We considered that if it was His will, we would find work, gain residency and stay permanently. If not, we would have had an amazing six-month adventure. Three years on we are still in New Zealand and are indeed permanent residents.

Now along this journey plenty of people had put questions in our minds – 'What about this, what about that?' – sowing doubt and creating distractions and obstacles in our path. It would have been so easy to listen to these things and set our minds into reasoning mode and shut God's voice out, but we chose to listen to God. Several good friends of ours had said, 'I don't think you will be coming back', which was confirmation of our own thinking. There will always be 'what if's?' in life but if we constantly reason and doubt then our human brain just takes over. The result is that we over-rationalise and can be in danger of missing all God has for us by doing nothing or not pursuing our dreams. Again, let peace be your guide and test.

So, we came, we found jobs, schools for the kids, found and bought a house, gained residency, all within *six months* of being in the country. Looking back on the timings of everything, they were perfect. We couldn't have orchestrated a move like that on our own if we had tried to. God was in control and we had to follow His leading. When the situation looked impossible, God made it possible. Now, don't get me wrong, it sounds easy when telling the story, but believe me there were plenty of stresses and obstacles along the way and definitely a sense of being out of our comfort zones. However, we focussed on what God had placed in us, pursued this and we had one thing – God with us and

God for us.

> *What then shall we say to these things? If God is for us, who can be against us?*
> (Romans 8:31, NKJV)

CHAPTER 7

Living The Lessons

July 2016 didn't get off to a good start for me.

Through this time of moving forward, having come through the valley, it was as if God was testing my faith further to see if I could apply the lessons I'd learned to everyday life.

All the time I had to ask myself;

- Have I stopped, looked and listened today?
- Have I applied the established good habits today?
- Am I choosing to live in joy today?
- Have I rested, reflected and renewed myself in God today?

The weeks that followed felt like testing times for me, as I had had a hideous gastric flare up the previous week, was struggling with an eye infection, back pain as well as hormonal migraines and cramps, all mixed in with the chronic nausea. This could have quickly had me back to square one. However, I am pleased to say it didn't completely debilitate me and get the better of me. It nearly did, but I noticed shifts in my thinking from these lessons that enabled me to take the rough with the smooth. Life is not always smooth; we just need to approach it with

God's eyes – with His perspective.

I had kept reminding myself – this is temporary. When I focussed on the symptoms (which took a lot of willpower not to) my joy and peace left me, I became anxious and my mind started to think of the 'what if's?' When I quickly got myself out of the negative thinking and my eyes off the situation and back on God, I was OK again. My body may not have been doing what I wanted it to do, but I was OK. God is on high and He was and is watching out for me. When we put life into perspective we have to remember that our bodies are ageing daily and we can expect to have ailments along the way, physically we are not invincible, we are human!

1. STOP, LOOK AND LISTEN

Reflecting on conversations with different people this week I started to think, what do we get from spending our whole lives rushing about, busying ourselves 24/7? Life shouldn't be a competition and real success is not measured by how much we are doing, whatever the world may say. When we get to heaven God will not say, 'Good, look how much you did'; He will want to know where He was in all that. Times and seasons come and go and we need to hear God's voice on what to do in those seasons. In this 'healing season' for me, I had to embrace the routine and listen to God and trust His timing in getting me back to full health. We can't rush God, it our job just to trust Him and believe Him.

2. ESTABLISH GOOD HABITS

Just at the right moment (25 July) a song recommendation popped into my inbox; *Live in the Wonderful* (2016, Lakewood Music).

This song would get me through the day and the week ahead as I meditated and worshipped through the words. The song reminded me to stay focused on God and see things through His eyes while I was waiting for my full healing.

This seamlessly tied in with a sermon on faith, I had heard at church the previous day. God is good in how He speaks to us and confirms things to us. The points that resonated with my spirit were;

- Sometimes healings aren't instant, they are a gradual process. That resonated in my spirit in praying for new discs and waiting for the old tissue to be broken down. I had been feeling fed up and discouraged as I had tried to ride a bike and it had set off my back pain/ inflammation, I realised how easy it was to declare negative comments from my mouth, in my case, about my back. As the preacher said, this is what we are *not* to do.
- We have to use wisdom in the healing process.
- We have to keep believing that God can do the supernatural in our healing.
- Naturally things can get better but God is SUPERNATURAL and can accelerate the process.
- There are lessons to be learned in the process and this is the test.
- Will we still believe for our miracle even when we don't see it instantly?
- Will we still declare our healing and move towards our breakthrough or will we get discouraged, despondent and depressed?

This believing and declaring is what I want for myself and others and I realised again that it all starts with our minds. We need to constantly renew our minds, renew our thinking and in these times only scripture will do; meditating on the Word of God day and night.

> *This Book of the Law shall not depart from your mouth, but you shall meditate in it day and night, that you may observe to do according to all that is written in it. For then you will make your way prosperous, and then you will have good success.* (Joshua 1:8, NKJV)

Meditating on the word of God day and night is what will get us through. If God lays a scripture on your heart for someone, then be obedient and share it with them no matter how insignificant you think it seems; it could be the most significant turning point for them in their breakthrough. It could be the change in direction of their thinking that is needed.

Anyway, back to the message. After I heard this I felt prompted to go forward for prayer for my new discs. Again, this was a prompting from God to put my faith into action as I felt like God was sorting out one thing at a time. First the undiagnosed virus symptoms, then the back and the little niggles in my body. It gave me hope that the gastric issues must be next! It's like God was fixing me in reverse order, with the longest issue (gastric) being the last to go.

3. LIVE IN JOY

One week on from receiving prayer (1 August) for new discs I was not back on the bike, but at the same time wasn't discouraged by this. I could have thought; 'I've had prayer for my back before, I've believed, I'm not back on my bike', but I didn't go down that route. I said, 'God what should I do?'

I felt God telling me to increase strength first, get my gastric issues solved and then the bike would come. Building up the walking is what I knew in my spirit that God was telling me to do; that is logical and wise. You don't just go blindly running a marathon one day – what do you do? You train, build up gradually until you reach the goal. On reflection and focussing on the positives God was doing in my body, I realised that I felt taller; a good sign I thought, that God was at work on the discs. I also managed several 40-minute brisk walks with no pain and ease of movement in my walking. I felt like I was walking 'normally' again. I went on a short beach walk which is up and down on different gradients (where in the past I would have experienced pain at some point) and no pain was present. When I walked I thanked God that He was putting my discs into place. Like a car you would bed in the brake discs, so that resonated in my spirit that this is what was going on in my body.

All the time I was continuing on through daily life with its pressures, and I had to continually remember to focus on Him and remember to 'live in joy', as it would be so easy to lose it, especially when feeling weary, due to the nausea, and other niggly issues. I had to make a conscious effort to thank God for what he was doing and continue to trust Him with my gastric issues that I had tried so hard to solve myself. I had to again reflect and look at how far I'd come and what God had already done. My virus symptoms were gone, my back getting stronger each day, those niggly things that once dragged me down were gone. I then had to be specific and continue to ask God to sort out the big issue - whatever might be going on in my gut. Without fuel from eating properly it was hard to get the energy to praise God, serve God, motivate myself, but in these situations we have to live in the supernatural and ask for His divine power. We need to focus on scripture and speak it out and declare it over our lives even when we can't see the miracle. I prayed that all the glory would go to God through what I faced in the valley and I had to keep this as my focus.

God was sorting out one problem at a time, so seeing the healings which had already taken place gave me hope that it would only be a matter of time before the other issues were also sorted.

Throughout the month of August God was continually reminding me of what I felt was the biggest of the lessons - to 'live in joy' and again I was taken back to the scripture in 2 Timothy 1:7 (12 August) when attending a women's conference. Interestingly this was one of the first scriptures to be quoted in the whole event and was again, confirmation of God speaking to me in my situation.

For God has not given us a spirit of fear, but of power, and of love and of a sound mind. (2 Timothy 1:7, NKJV)

Reflecting on all the messages I had received from the women's conference 'She Carries' (Whanganui 2016) raised a lot of questions in my mind. What am I wearing? What haven't I forgiven myself for? What am I holding onto? As the message said, in summary; *Christ paid so forgiveness is a free gift; all we have to do is accept it. We are not worthy but Christ decided we were and paid for us all. It is us that has to forgive ourselves and let go of the memories that cause pain so that we can live in freedom, peace and joy.*

One speaker reminded us that we need to take off the burkha of shame, condemnation, whatever it may be and forgive ourselves; righteousness, peace and joy are the evidence of freedom.

...for the kingdom of God is not eating and drinking, but righteousness and peace and joy in the Holy Spirit. (Romans 14:17, NKJV)

I realised that I had to get serious with God and address any issues that may be hindering me living in joy. That is deeply personal between us and God and we all have different things we carry around. The important thing is to let God highlight them and then deal with them and then we can move forward into everything He has for us.

4. REST, REFLECT, RENEW

The rest, reflect, renew lesson was one of the hardest to incorporate in everyday life, but at the same time the most powerful. The following words document the resting, reflections and renewal and the revelations that came to me in these times.

- I learned that if we take the time to really be still and focus in on God, we will hear all that He is saying to us and see Him guiding us each step of the way through our lives. In these times I became amazed at how much God was saying to me and realised that I really did need to open my ears!

- I started to take time to listen to what God was saying by making weekly trips to the 'mountain view' and walks around the lake. These became two places where I could really find God and 'be still' with no distraction, expecting to hear from God.

- It may not have been cycling twenty km but it was a new found place and the realisation came that we can find God anywhere if we just tune into Him and his presence, which is continually with us. These became places where I could say, 'Speak, God, for your servant is listening.' Just as Samuel finally realised it was God speaking, so we too have to find a place where we can really hear God and just focus in on Him.

Now the Lord came and stood and called as at other times, "Samuel! Samuel!" And Samuel answered, "Speak, for your servant hears." (1 Samuel 3:10, NKJV)

I was prompted to write some of these revelations down, which will follow on in the appendix, as a source of inspiration/encouragement as you seek God in your own life.

The end?

Now, when thinking of the ending of this journey/book, I came to the realisation that there wouldn't actually be an ending as such, as there will always be trials in life. I realised that the ending wouldn't be the important thing; it would be the process of renewing of the mind and the application of the lessons.

A trial will always end in victory, whether that victory be physical healing, emotional healing, spiritual healing, a calling home. Whatever it is, find God in the midst of your trial, find out what He is saying to you, embrace the change/lessons, move forward into victory and apply what you have learnt. Doing this allows us to live in victory whatever the circumstances. Whatever valleys we then face in life, we will be able to tackle head on with Godly confidence and not keep going round the mountain on some issues.

In closing, wherever you are in your valley, I pray that the four-part lesson that God taught me in my valley will help you move further through yours.

1. Stop, look and listen – Have I today?
2. Establish good habits – Have I worshipped, read the Word, talked to God today?
3. Live in joy – Am I choosing to live in joy today?
4. Rest, reflect and renew – Have I rested, reflected and renewed myself in God today?

Take what you have read, move forward through your valley with

God, with your unique tools to get you through. Remember, God will always get you through the valley and out the other side.

Appendix Of Revelations

Following are some of the revelations that came as I applied the lessons learned in the valley (Chapter 7).

REVELATION

Whilst sitting waiting in the car looking out onto the hills and river; and waiting on God (2 August) needing Him to speak to me/guide me, God gave me several words to research:

- Water
- River
- Mountain
- See.

The words that then came into my spirit as I was still were; 'I (God) am a tree of life and I (me) am like a tree planted by the water.'

I looked up scripture references involving these words on my return home and several resonated with my spirit.

Behold, I will do a new thing, Now it shall spring forth; Shall you not know it? I will even make a road in the wilderness and rivers in the desert.

(Isaiah 43:19, NKJV)

Then He turned to His disciples and said privately, "Blessed are the eyes which see the things you see... (Luke 10:23, NKJV)

She is a tree of life to those who take hold of her, and happy are all who retain her. (Proverbs 3:18, NKJV)

He shall be like a tree planted by the rivers of water, that brings forth its fruit in its season, whose leaf also shall not wither; and whatever he does shall prosper. (Psalms 1:3, NKJV)

The grass withers, the flower fades, but the word of our God stands forever. (Isaiah 40:8, NKJV)

Who has measured the waters in the hollow of His hand, measured heaven with a span and calculated the dust of the earth in a measure? Weighed the mountains in scales and the hills in a balance? (Isaiah 40:12, NKJV)

I will open rivers in desolate heights, and fountains in the midst of the valleys; I will make the wilderness a pool of water, and the dry land springs of water. 19 I will plant in the wilderness the cedar and the acacia tree, the myrtle and the oil tree; I will set in the desert the cypress tree and the pine and the box tree together, 20 that they may see and know, and consider and understand together, that the hand of the LORD has done this, and the Holy One of Israel has created it. (Isaiah 41:18-20, NKJV)

Let the sea roar, and all its fullness, the world and those who dwell in it; 8 let the rivers clap their hands; let the hills be joyful together before the LORD. (Psalms 98:7-8, NKJV)

REVELATION

Once when walking around the lake and listening to the inspirational worship music on my iPod, the song *'I Surrender All'* was playing and I started to pray out to God and challenged myself. Have I really surrendered all to God? What does that actually mean? I realised it meant to let go/loosen my grip and cease control.

I surrender – past relationships

I surrender – anger

I surrender – language

I surrender – my time

I surrender – my teaching skills

I surrender – my writing skills

I surrender – my marriage

I surrender – my children

I surrender – church

As I walked on, the sun was shining bright like diamonds on the lake. In my spirit the words, 'In heaven they will be real diamonds', a promise to come and a reminder that this life is temporary.

REVELATION

Today my mind was taken back to the revelation at the start of the valley: Everything written (by the spirit) will turn to gold and the instruction to write my way out of the valley.

The words 'gold souls' popped into my spirit and confirmed in my spirit the reason for the book and that souls are more important and valuable than real gold. This inspired me to keep going and to keep writing as I was nearing the end of the book.

REVELATION – MOUNTAIN VIEW

Looking out to the distant mountain and hills over the Whanganui River, words came into my spirit so I wrote them down.

The same view, viewed by the same eyes doesn't always appear the same.

The mountain hasn't moved, I haven't moved but God- controlled environmental factors make the view look different each time.

In the same way, as the seasons come and go and the weather in our lives changes, so will the view (of our circumstances).

Remember, God has not moved, he is changing our view of something by changing things in and around us. The constant 'Him' remains the same.

Jesus Christ is the same yesterday, today and forever. (Hebrews 13:8, NKJV)

REVELATION

Today, I was reminded of the free gift of forgiveness from God to us.

Now we have received, not the spirit of the world, but the spirit who is from God, that we might know the things that have been freely given to us by God.
(1 Corinthians 2:12, NKJV)

God freely gives us the gift of forgiveness – we just have to accept it.

We live by the spirit, not by worldly expectations.

REVELATION

Beside the lake today I stopped to look at the fountain and the following revelations came.

- I am the fountain of life.
- Mist – here I am in the midst of you.
- Continually be filled with the Holy Spirit as life makes you leak.
- My spirit will pour forth from you.
- No ceilings for the fountain/in how high it/you can go. *No* limits.

On research through scriptures I felt a resonating to combine with these revelations.

For the Lamb who is in the midst of the throne will shepherd them and lead them to living fountains of waters. And God will wipe away every tear from their eyes. (Revelation 7:17, NKJV).

And the disciples were filled with joy and with the Holy Spirit. (Acts 13:52, NKJV)

"...but whoever drinks of the water that I shall give him will never thirst. But the water that I shall give him will become in him a fountain of water springing up into everlasting life." (John 4:14, NKJV)

REVELATION

The joy of the Lord is your strength.

(Nehemiah 8:10, NKJV)

With natural water and natural thinking you will become thirsty again but with Me you will never be thirsty.

Jesus answered and said to her, "Whoever drinks of this water will thirst again, but whoever drinks of the water that I shall give him will never thirst."

(John 4:13-14 NKJV)

If you are thirsty, you need to drink Him in. This is not just a one-time thing. When you feel your joy being depleted by circumstances then drink again and let your fountain burst forth. Drinking can be through worship, word, prayer, and all the time focussing your attention on Him /listening to Him and being truly still.

REVELATION- LAKE WALK

I saw the sun shining on the lake as it began to break-through the haze and was then reflected on the water.

This sun trying to break through the haze was significant as it reminded me exactly of a picture I had taken of the same thing at home on 27 May which had marked my healing and coming out of the valley.

The sun also appeared as the moon today reflecting light as it was breaking through the haze.

Scriptures to go with these revelations;

He appointed the moon for seasons;

The sun knows its going down. (Psalms 104:19, NKJV)

Like the hazy sun (which had appearance like the moon) hovering over the lake in my revelation, so it reminded me of the scripture when God formed the world.

The earth was without form, and void; and darkness was on the face of the deep. And the Spirit of God was hovering over the face of the waters. (Genesis 1:2 (NKJV)

The resonation in my spirit was that this was the season and God would continue to keep breaking through for me.

You may look up and all looks grey but behind you the sun is trying to break through the cloud – so God is watching over you/has got your back and will break through for you at the right and perfect time.

REVELATION

Today God gave me two words; Fear and Protection.

- Fear – No fear for children of God.

Confirmation of this through song lyrics heard on the radio; 'I am no longer a slave to fear-I am a child of God,' and scripture revelation.

There is no fear in love; but perfect love casts out fear, because fear involves tor-

ment. But he who fears has not been made perfect in love. (1 John 4:18, **NKJV**)

- Protection

On my lake walk I encountered a bird protecting her nest.

The resonating in my spirit that God has a circle of protection around us wherever we go. The devil can't touch us. Just as the bird at the lake had created a circle of protection around its nest, so God does this for us, His children.

www.ingramcontent.com/pod-product-compliance
Lightning Source LLC
Chambersburg PA
CBHW060355180626
46817CB00008B/3028